100
PRETENTIOUS
NURSERY RHYMES

First published 2002, reprinted in 2003 by
Prion Books Limited
an imprint of the Carlton Publishing Group
20 Mortimer Street
london W1T 3JW

ISBN 1-85375-487 0

Cover design by Grade Design

Printed and bound in Great Britain
by Bookmarque, Croydon, Surrey

100
PRETENTIOUS
NURSERY RHYMES

by Michael Powell

PRION

A jumper of ditches,
A leaper of thorns,
A little grey man with
Two leather horns.

*An achromatic midget skilled
at saltation
Of long narrow trenches used
for irrigation,
And modified branches with spines on
the side,
Has cranial protuberances of dressed or
tanned hide.*

Baa baa black sheep
Have you any wool?
Yes sir, yes sir, three bags full.
One for the master,
One for the dame,
And one for the little boy
Who lives down the lane.

Ululate ululate, sable ewe,
Is there any wool in your purlieu?
Ipso facto I concede
Three Prada handbags stuffed indeed.
One for the master,
One for the dame,
And one for a male progeny who
resides down a narrow country lane.

Barber, barber, shave a pig!
How many hairs to make a wig?
Four and twenty, that's enough!
Give the barber a pinch of snuff.

*Barber, cause Sus scrofa domesticus'
hispidity to cease!
How many capillaments to construct a
rudimentary hairpiece?
Four and twenty should complete
the operation!
Offer the barber a finely-pulverized
tobacco preparation.*

Bat, bat, come under my hat,
And I'll give you a slice of bacon;
And when I bake
I'll give you a cake,
If I am not mistaken.

Bat, Bat, Come Under My Hat

Nocturnal flying mammal of the order
Chiroptera, go
Underneath my chapeau.
To you I will donate thin broad pieces
of salted and smoked pig meat;
And when I cook with dry heat:
A sweet baked food made of flour, liquid
and eggs in combination;
Unless I have misapprehended
the situation.

Bobby Shaftoe went to sea,
Silver buckles on his knee.
He'll come back and marry me,
Pretty Bobby Shaftoe.

Bobby Shaftoe's fine and fair,
Combing down his auburn hair.
He's my friend for evermore,
Pretty Bobby Shaftoe.

Bobby Shaftoe is a nautical chap,
He has a lustrous white, ductile,
malleable metallic fastening on
his kneecap.
He will debark for our nuptials asap:
What a beau, Bobby Shaftoe.

Bobby Shaftoe deserves
much admiration,
Arranging his coiffure of
auburn colouration.
In sempiternity we shall enjoy
close association:
What a beau, Bobby Shaftoe.

Boys and girls, come out to play.
The moon doth shine as bright
as day!
Leave your supper and leave
your sleep,
And come with your playfellows
into the street.
Come with a whistle,
Come with a call,
Come with good will, or not at all.

*Children, participate in outdoor
recreational indulgence.
The Orb of Night reflects light of
quasi-solar effulgence!
Relinquish your repast and your
nocturnal reveries:
Enjoy leisure pursuits with
your contemporaries.
Purse your lips to create a shrill sound,
Approach with stentorian tone,
Display magnanimity or else
remain at home.*

Bye, baby bunting,
Daddy's gone a-hunting,
Gone to get a rabbit skin
To wrap the baby bunting in.

Farewell, you miracle of creation,
Your paternal progenitor indulges
in venation,
To locate a long-eared, short-tailed,
burrowing mammal to flay,
To afford you comfortable
swaddling today.

Christmas is coming,
The geese are getting fat,
Please to put a penny
In the old man's hat.
If you haven't got a penny,
A ha'penny will do;
If you haven't got a ha'penny,
Then God bless you!

Yuletide is approaching,
Water fowl begin to grow,
Kindly place a small oblation
In the patriarch's chapeau.
Just a small donation,
Or half this sum will do;
If you're financially insolvent
Then God bless you!

Cobbler, cobbler, mend my shoe.
Get it done by half past two.
Half past two is much too late!
Get it done by half past eight.
Stitch it up, and stitch it down,
And I'll give you a half a crown.

Cobbler, Cobbler, Mend My Shoe

Cobbler, perform a repair
On my footwear.
And here's the crunch:
I need them back after lunch.
No, after a moment's thought
That last remark I must abort;
That was a ballpark approximation.
I have revised my estimation
and hereby give you advance warning:
I actually need it by the morning.
So if you could, it would
be much appreciated
And of course you will be remunerated.
Cheers.

Daffy Down Dilly
Has come to town
In a yellow petticoat
And a green gown.

Resplendent in a saffron petticoat and
Pashmina of verdant hue,
(that portion of the visible spectrum
which lies between yellow and blue),
Daffy Down Dilly prepares to enter
The town centre.

Dance to your Daddy,
My little babby,
Dance to your Daddy,
My little lamb.
You shall have a fishy
In a little dishy,
You shall have a fishy
When the boat comes in.

Move rhythmically using prescribed or
improvised step and gesture
To entertain your male progenitor.
Move rhythmically using prescribed or
improvised step and gesture
My immediate descendant,
My baby sheep.
You will have a Dover Sole
In a tiny Wedgwood bowl,
You will have a Dover Sole
When the boat comes in.

Davy Davy Dumpling,
Boil him in a pot;
Sugar him, and butter him,
And eat him while he's hot!

***

Diddle, diddle dumpling,
my son John.
Went to bed with his trousers on,
One shoe off, and one shoe on,
Diddle, diddle dumpling,
my son John.

Davy Davy Dumpling,
Occasion ebullition;
Dulcify and lubricate,
For torrid deglutition.

***

Diddle, diddle dumpling,
my son Jeremy,
Went to bed wearing trousers designed
by Wayne Hemingway
And a single polished calfskin brogue
with gold filigree,
Diddle, diddle dumpling,
my son Jeremy.

Ding, dong, bell,
Pussy's in the well.
Who put her in?
Little Johnny Green.
Who pulled her out?
Little Tommy Stout.
What a naughty boy was that,
To try to drown poor pussy cat,
Who never did him any harm,
And killed the mice in his
father's barn.

Ding, Dong, Bell

A hollow musical instrument
reverberates with a metallic sound;
In a deep shaft a moribund cat can
be found.
Who is responsible for this
crime scene?
Diminutive Johnny Green.
Who pulled her out?
Diminutive Tommy Stout.
How improper to thus trammel
A small carnivorous
domesticated mammal;
who innocuously fulfilled an
important role
In rodent pest control.

I do not like thee, Doctor Fell,
The reason why, I cannot tell;
But this I know, and know full well,
I do not like thee, Doctor Fell.

*Doctor Fell, for you I have a
nebulous feeling of disdain
The reason for which I cannot fully
ascertain.
But I am confident, following
empirical observation,
That you are an object of execration.*

Doctor Foster went to Gloucester
In a shower of rain.
He stepped in a puddle
Right up to his middle,
And never went there again.

Doctor Foster went to Gloucester
At a time of ethereal volatility.
A puddle he stepped in
Reached his sacral meridian,
And he never returned to the city.

Elsie Marley's grown so fine,
She won't get up to feed the swine,
But lies in bed 'till eight or nine!
Lazy Elsie Marley.

Elsie Marley has become so
presumptuously arrogant,
She neglects to administer
porcine nourishment;
She is matutinally indolent!
Lethargic Elsie Marley.

Fee, Fie, Foh, Fum!
I smell the blood of an Englishman:
Be he alive or be he dead,
I'll grind his bones to make
my bread.

Fee, Fie, Foh, Fum!
I smell the blood of an Englishman:
Be he alive or be he dead,
I'll reduce his dense, semi-rigid,
porous, calcified connective tissue
To finely dispersed solid particles by
friction in order to make
A staple food using flour or meal mixed
with other dry and liquid ingredients
Combined with a leavening agent,
which I'll knead and bake.

Every lady in this land
Has five nails upon each hand,
Twenty on her hands and feet;
All this is true, without deceit.

Five Nails

*Upon each terminal part of her upper
limbs every lady in this land luxuriates
In five transparent keratinous plates;
On all her appendages a total
of twenty;
This number will stand up to scrutiny.*

Four ducks on a pond,
A grass bank beyond,
A blue sky of spring,
White clouds on the wing:
What a little thing
To remember for years,
To remember with tears!

Of the family Anatidae, four warm-
blooded, egg-laying, feathered vertebrates
Were swimming on a still body of
water smaller than a lake,
Beneath a steep natural incline of fescue,
The upper atmosphere as seen from the
Earth's surface is the hue
Of that portion of the visible spectrum
lying between
Indigo and green;
Visible bodies of fine water droplets the
achromatic colour of maximum
illumination.
What a trifling location
To remember for so long a duration
With drops of a lachrymation.

Fuzzy Wuzzy was a bear,
Fuzzy Wuzzy had no hair,
Fuzzy Wuzzy wasn't fuzzy,
Was he?

*An omnivorous mammal of the
family Ursidae,
Fuzzy Wuzzy was its moniker.
Fuzzy Wuzzy was as bald as a coot,
Fuzzy Wuzzy wasn't hirsute.
Was he?*

Georgie Porgie pudding and pie
Kissed the girls and made them cry.
When the girls come out to play
Georgie Porgie runs away.

Georgie Porgie sorbet and vol-au-vent,
Offered osculation that the girls didn't want.
When they beguile the time with merry recreation,
Georgie Porgie uses tactical evasion.

Now all of you, give heed unto
The tale I now relate,
About two girls and one small boy,
A cat, and a green gate.
Alack! Since I began to speak . . .
And what I say is true . . .
It's all gone out of my poor head.
And so good-bye to you!

*Pay attention while I recount a tale
Of three children, only one of
whom was male,
And what's more:
F. domesticus: a small
mammalian carnivore
And a portal creation of
green coloration. Eheu!
Amnesia obliges me to bid you
all adieu.*

Good night, sleep tight,
Don't let the bedbugs bite
Wake up bright
In the morning light
To do what's right
With all your might.

As the jaws of darkness close,
visit Morpheus' bower in
saccharine repose.
Do not permit Cimex lectularius to
pierce your tegument;
Awake with a deep feeling of content,
As you bid farewell to
nocturnal opacity,
Adopt an attitude
of fervent rectitude.

Head, shoulders, knees and toes,
Knees and toes.
Head, shoulders, knees and toes,
Knees and toes.
And eyes, and ears, and mouth,
and nose.
Head, shoulders, knees and toes,
Knees and toes.

*Cranium, glenoid fossa, patella
and phalanges,
Patella and phalanges.
Cranium, glenoid fossa, patella
and phalanges,
Patella and phalanges.
And bulbus oculi, auricle, oral cavity
and olfactory organ.
Cranium, glenoid fossa, patella
and phalanges,
Patella and phalanges.*

Hey diddle diddle, the cat and
the fiddle
The cow jumped over the moon.
The little dog laughed to see
such fun
And the dish ran away with
the spoon.

Hey diddle diddle, felis and fiddle
A heifer vaulted the Orb of Night,
While a runtish and ludibrious hound
Saw sundry tableware take flight.

Hickory, dickory, dock,
The mouse ran up the clock;
The clock struck one,
The mouse ran down,
Hickory, dickory, dock.

Hickory, dickory, dock,
The rodent ascended the clock;
A chronometrical peal
Mitigated its zeal,
Hickory, dickory, dock.

Higglety, pigglety, my black hen,
She lays eggs for gentlemen.
Gentlemen come every day
To see what my black hen doth lay.
Sometimes nine, and
sometimes ten.
Higglety, pigglety, my black hen.

Higglety, pigglety, my
sable-vested hen,
She ovulates for gentlemen.
The haut monde form a daily lobby,
To scrutinize each oval
reproductive body.
Sometimes nine and sometimes ten.
Higglety, pigglety, my
sable-vested hen.

Horsie, horsie, don't you stop,
Just let your feet go clippety clop;
Your tail goes swish,
And the wheels go 'round,
Giddyup, you're homeward bound!

Horsie, Horsie, Don't You Stop

On, on you noble steed!
With a thousand clips and quivering
clops, may your horny
extremities proceed.
Your tail goes swish,
The wheels delight in their
sublime rotation,
Pray do not tarry on your
homeward migration.

Humpty Dumpty sat on the wall
Humpty Dumpty had a great fall.
All the king's horses and all the
king's men
Couldn't put Humpty together
again.

*Humpty Dumpty eschewed concavity
When, sitting on a wall, he succumbed
to gravity.
Imperial equine and human assistance
Could not restore Humpty to his
ovoid consistence.*

Hush-a-bye, baby, on the treetop,
When the wind blows the cradle
will rock;
When the bough breaks the cradle
will fall,
Down will come baby, cradle
and all.

*Hush-a-bye baby, swathed in
arboreal vegetation,
The zephyrous pressure will
kindle vacillation,
Causing the cradle to plunge from
the ramage
And suffer significant damage.*

I had a little husband
no bigger than my thumb;
I put him in a pint pot
And there I bid him drum.
I bought a little handkerchief
to wipe his little nose,
And a pair of little garters
to tie his little hose.
I bought a little horse
that galloped up and down;
I bridled him and saddled him
and sent him out of town.

I Had A Little Husband

I was married to a midget
No bigger than my opposable digit.
I placed him in a drinking vessel
And bid him percussively fidget.
For a small square of cloth I spared
no expense
To lightly rub his tiny
nasal protuberance.
Two elasticized bands I also bought
To provide hosiery support.
Then I procured with further money
A hyperactive Shetland pony.
I added a restraint and a seat made
of leather,
And the horse carried him out of my
life for ever.

I heard a horseman
Ride over the hill;
The moon shone clear,
The night was still;
His helm was silver,
And pale was he;
And the horse he rode
Was of ivory.

*I perceived the sound of a man skilled
in equitation,
Riding over a well-defined
geographical formation;
The Earth's biggest natural satellite,
Free from clouds, mist, or haze,
shone bright;
The period between sunset and sunrise
was free from disturbance
and movement;
His headwear was of a lustrous,
ductile, malleable metallic element;
He was whitish in complexion and his
equine mammal
Was composed of enamel.*

If I had a donkey
That wouldn't go
Do you think I'd beat him?
Oh, no, no!
I'd put him in a barn
And give him some corn,
The best little donkey
That ever was born.

If I had a beast of burden
Behaving cataleptically,
Any form of punishment
I would view most sceptically.
I would put him in a barn and
Offer cereal grass
To my peerless ass.

I'm a little teapot
Short and stout
Here is my handle
Here is my spout.
When I get all steamed up
Hear me shout:
Tip me up
and pour me out!

I'm A Little Teapot

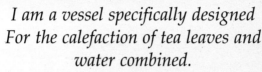

I am a vessel specifically designed
For the calefaction of tea leaves and
water combined.
I am of diminutive dimension:
A corpulent invention.
Observe the place where your hand is
supposed to go.
Observe the outlet where the drink is
supposed to flow.
When my temperature is high,
Ebullition will make me cry:
You must use leverage
To release the beverage.

Incy-wincy spider
Climbed up the waterspout
Down came the rain
And washed the spider out.
Out came the sun
And dried up all the rain
So the incy-wincy spider
Climbed up the spout again!

*A diminutive arachnid a
conduit surmounted;
After much precipitation the
spider dismounted.
The sun's luminescence caused
substantial desiccation;
The intrepid creature achieved
its aspiration.*

Jack and Jill went up the hill
To fetch a pail of water;
Jack fell down and broke his crown
And Jill came tumbling after.

Jack and Jill ascended the hill,
To fetch some mineral water;
Jack's titubation caused
pericranial vitiation;
Jill emulated him shortly after.

Jack be nimble
Jack be quick
Jack jump over
The candlestick.

Jack be nimble
Jack hie at once
Jack saltate
Over yonder sconce.

Jack Sprat could eat no fat,
His wife could eat no lean,
And so between them both,
you see,
They licked the platter clean.

Jack Sprat ate food that was fat free,
Although his wife
behaved diametrically.
By exploiting their disparity of
gastronomic taste,
Their co-dependence ensured the
minimum of waste.

Handy Pandy, Jack-a-Dandy,
Loves plum-cake and sugar-candy:
He bought some at a grocer's shop,
And out he came,
hop, hop, hop, hop.

Handy Pandy, Jack-a-Dandy,
Loves a sweet baked food of flour,
liquid, eggs, plum cake and
crystalline disaccharide-candy:
He bought some at a purveyor of
fruit and veg,
Which he egressed using a single
lower appendage.

Here am I, little Jumping Joan;
When nobody's with me
I'm always alone.

Here am I, little Jumping Joan;
When nobody's with me
I'm always alone.
(Or, as a phenomenalist,
Do I cease to exist?)

Ladybird! Ladybird!
Fly away home.
Your house is on fire
And your children all gone.
All except one,
And that's little Ann,
For she has crept under
The frying pan.

Red aphid-eater with black punctation!
Avolate to your domestic conflagration.
All your progeny have decamped
And little Ann is extremely cramped:
Instead of running away
She's under the Le Creuset.

Little Betty Blue lost her
holiday shoe.
What can little Betty do?
Give her another, to match
the other,
And then she may walk in two.

*Little Betty Blue was unsuccessful in
retaining possession of one of a pair
Of leisure footwear.
What strategy should this negligent
female adopt?
Offer her another, to supersede the one
she dropped.*

Little Bo-Peep has lost her sheep,
And can't tell where to find them.
Leave them alone, and they'll
come home.
Wagging their tales behind them.

*Little Bo-Peep has demonstrably failed
in her mission
To maintain a group of ruminant
mammals under close supervision.
At home the animals will
happily reappear,
So long as Bo-Peep doesn't interfere.*

Little Boy Blue, come blow
your horn.
The sheep's in the meadow, the
cow's in the corn.
Where is the boy who looks after
the sheep?
He's under the haystack fast asleep!

Little Boy with cerulescent aura,
Make use of your pulmonic bravura:
In a tract of pasture the
horned ruminant
Of the genus Ovis is clearly extant.
The female bovine, sans horn
Is situated in the corn.
Apprise me of the boy's location,
(the one entrusted with an
ovine vocation).
He is subjacent to a large stack of hay,
Flat on his back and snoring away.

What are little boys made of?
Snips and snails,
And puppy dog tails,
That's what little boys are made of.

After chemical analysis
data was compiled,
Regarding the constituent components
of a male child:
A posterior canine
appendage, gastropods
And various other unidentified
odds and sods.

What are little girls made of?
Sugar and spice,
And everything nice,
That's what little girls are made of.

*After similar analysis
data was compiled,
Regarding the constituent components
of a female child:
Pungent aromatic plant matter and a
water-soluble crystalline disaccharide,
And everything agreeable was
detected inside.*

Little Jack Horner
Sat in the corner,
Eating a Christmas pie;
He put in his thumb,
And pulled out a plum,
And said, 'what a good boy am I!'

Little Jack Horner

Little Jack Horner liked to eat
Christmas pie where two walls meet.
His phalangeal dexterity was so acute
He deftly retrieved a small purple fruit,
And then sought to impress,
By boasting of his success.

Little Miss Muffet sat on a tuffet,
Eating some curds and whey.
Along came a spider
And sat down beside her,
And frightened Miss Muffet away.

Little Miss Muffet sat on a tuffet,
Enjoying her milky repast.
An arachnid's arrival
Threatened her survival,
So she left, to avoid being harassed.

Little Robin Redbreast sat
upon a tree,
Up went Pussy-Cat, down went he,
Down came Pussy-Cat, away
Robin ran,
Says little Robin Redbreast: 'Catch
me if you can!'

Little Robin Redbreast jumped
upon a spade,
Pussy-Cat jumped after him, and
then he was afraid.
Little Robin chirped and sang, and
what did Pussy say?
Pussy-Cat said: 'Mew, mew, mew,'
and Robin flew away.

Erithacus rubecula in arboreal location.
A feline foe caused his declination.
Fleeing, he taunted his antagonist
With his prowess as an evasion specialist.
The fugitive mounted a tool
for excavation.
His assailant's approach caused him
trepidation.
As a displacement activity, he started
to cantate,
The cat vocalised, the bird began
to aviate.

Little Tommy Tucker
Sings for his supper:
What shall he eat?
White bread and butter.
How shall he cut it
Without a knife?
How can he marry
Without a wife?

Little Tommy Tucker
Extemporizes for his supper.
What shall he take into his body
for digestion?
Bruschetta and animal fat is
my suggestion.
Without a sharp cutting edge
How shall he separate the bread?
And without a helpmate
How shall he be wed?

Little Tommy Tittlemouse
Lived in a little house;
He caught fishes
In other men's ditches.

Little Tommy Tittlemouse
Resided in a little house;
He cast his bait
On other men's real estate.

Lizzie Borden took an axe
And gave her mother forty whacks.
And when she saw what she
had done,
She gave her father forty-one.

*Using a tool with a heavy-headed blade
mounted crosswise on a shaft of wood,
Lizzie Borden violently inveighed
against motherhood.
Then fully cognisant of her actions,
this delinquent daughter
Indulged in further parental slaughter.*

Mary had a little lamb,
Its fleece was white as snow;
And everywhere that Mary went
The lamb was sure to go.

Mary had a callow sheep
With pellicule of niveous hue;
Ubiquitous though Mary was
It was inured to pursue.

Mary, Mary quite contrary,
How does your garden grow?
With silver bells and cockle-shells
And pretty maids all in a row.

Mary, Mary with
recalcitrant demeanour,
Kindly reveal your eclectic
agricultural schema.
I make argent cup-shaped metal
instruments resonate
While combining a row of beauty
queens with calcium carbonate.

Mother, may I go out to swim?
Yes, my darling daughter.
Hang your clothes on a
hickory limb,
But don't go near the water!

Mother, May I Go Out To Swim?

Mother, may I perform natation?
My dearly beloved female descendant,
you have my affirmation.
Your vestments should be attached
from above with no support
from below,
To a hickory branch, but eschew
the H_2O.

My Bonnie lies over the ocean,
My Bonnie lies over the sea.
My Bonnie lies over the ocean,
Please bring back my Bonnie to me.
Bring back,
Bring back,
Oh, bring back my Bonnie to me,
to me.
Bring back,
Bring back,
Oh, bring back my Bonnie to me.

My Bonnie lies over the ocean,
She's really quite an item.
Please assist her homeward motion:
Repeat ad infinitum.

As I was sitting in my chair,
I knew the bottom wasn't there,
Nor legs nor back, but I just sat,
Ignoring little things like that.

*As I was resting in a
sedentary position,
I had sudden cognition that
The chair
Wasn't there.
Yet I had scant appreciation
Of my extraordinary powers
of levitation.*

Hey, my kitten, my kitten,
And hey, my kitten, my deary;
Such a sweet pet as this
Was neither fat nor weary.

Hey, my kitten, my kitten,
And hey, my kitten, with all my
love imbued;
Such an endearing domesticated
animal as this
Suffered neither obesity nor physical or
mental lassitude.

Old King Cole was a merry
old soul,
And a merry old soul was he.
He called for his pipe,
And he called for his drum.
And he called for his fiddlers three.

Old King Cole

Old King Cole was a congenial soul;
Congeniality was his middle name.
He called for his ocarina,
He commissioned a tattoo
And he requisitioned a string trio of
high acclaim.

Old Mother Goose,
When she wanted to wander,
Would ride through the air
On a very fine gander.

*On those occasions when a matriarchal
water bird was inclined to meander,
She was accustomed to chartering a
superior gander.*

Old Mother Hubbard
Went to the cupboard
To get her poor dog a bone;
But when she came there
The cupboard was bare,
And so the poor dog had none.

Old Mother Hubbard

Old Mother Hubbard
Went to the cupboard
For a bone for her Pointing Griffon;
But when she came there
The cupboard was bare,
So her pedigree gun dog had none.

Once there was a little boy,
He lives in his skin;
When he pops out,
You may pop in.

Once there was a male child,
He lives within his integumentary
tissue membranes.
When he eviscerates himself,
You may inhabit his remains.

One, two, three, four, five,
Once I caught a fish alive,
Six, seven, eight, nine, ten,
Then I let it go again.
Why did you let it go?
Because it bit my finger so.
Which finger did it bite?
This little finger on the right.

One, two, three, four, five,
Once I caught a fish alive,
Six, seven, eight, nine, ten,
Then I let it go again.
Why did you liberate
This cold-blooded aquatic vertebrate?
After I received an excruciating bite,
I could no longer hold it tight.
On which digit did you sustain
This acute phalangeal pain?
I understand
It's the fifth finger on my right hand.

Pat-a-cake, pat-a-cake, baker's man
Bake me a cake as fast as you can;
Pat it and prick it and mark
it with B,
Put it in the oven for Baby and me.

Pat-a-cake, pat-a-cake,
baker's subsidiary.
Expedite for me a piece of
dough-based confectionery;
Stimulate, empierce and inscribe
the letter B,
Commit it to the Aga for the
weanling and me.

Peter, Peter, pumpkin eater
Had a wife and couldn't keep her,
He put her in a pumpkin shell,
And there he kept her very well.
Peter, Peter, pumpkin-eater,
Had another and didn't love her.
Peter learned to read and spell,
And then he loved her very well.

*An illiterate bygamist failed in his
matrimonial function
By housing his first wife in a pumpkin,
without the slightest compunction.
To his second he showed a similar lack
of consideration,
Until he had achieved a
rudimentary education.*

All around the mulberry bush
The monkey chased the weasel.
The monkey thought it was
such fun,
Pop! goes the weasel.
Half a pound of tupenny rice,
Half a pound of treacle,
That's the way the money goes,
Pop! goes the weasel.

Around a deciduous tree bearing
edible fruit
A weasel ran, with a medium-sized
primate in hot pursuit.
The latter enjoyed chasing around,
Until his small, slender-bodied
companion burst open with a sharp,
explosive sound.
226.796 grammes of inexpensive
edible grain
And a viscous derivative of sugarcane,
Such is the nature of finance and
capital trusts,
This time the weasel
spontaneously combusts.

Punch and Judy
Fought for a pie;
Punch gave Judy
A knock in the eye.
Says Punch to Judy:
'Will you have any more?'
Says Judy to Punch:
'My eye is too sore.'

*Punch resorted to his customary
aggression,
To ensure a baked food of filled pastry
remained in his possession;
In the violent confusion
Judy received an ocular contusion.
Her husband made a peace offering of a
piece of pastry of her choosing,
Which she declined due to
extensive bruising.*

Pussycat, pussycat,
Where have you been?
I've been to London
To visit the Queen.

Pussycat, pussycat,
What did you there?
I frightened a little mouse
Under her chair.

Pussycat, pussycat,
Whither do you peregrinate?
I've been to London
To visit a potentate.

Pussycat, pussycat,
What was your activity?
I terrorized a rodent
Under the monarch's posteriority.

Rain, rain, go away,
Come back another day.

I command those numerous spherical
globules to disappear
Instead of moving under the influence
of gravity from the Earth's
upper atmosphere –
Condensing from vapour as a clear,
colourless, odourless, and tasteless
liquid, H_2O –
To make contact with the land surface
of the world below.
Suspend the aforementioned
precipitant practice
Until the planet has completed at least
one rotation on its axis.

Red sky at night,
Shepherd's delight;
Red sky in the morning,
Shepherd's warning.

When nocturnal celestial regions
Are the colour of the long-wave end of
the visible spectrum,
A guardian of sheep is gleesome;
The same in a matutinal position:
A guardian of sheep offers
stern admonition.

Ring around the rosie,
A pocket full of posies,
Atishoo! Atishoo!
We all fall down.

***

Round and round the garden,
Like a teddy bear.
One step, two step,
Tickle you under there!

Around The Rosie/Round The Garden

Circumvent the ornamental shrub with
a prickly stem,
A pouch replete with flowers (idem).
Sternutation upon sternutation
Causes our sudden declination.

***

Round and round the garden,
Like a teddy bear.
Two complete movements of raising a
foot and putting it down,
Titillate you under there!

Row, row, row your boat
Gently down the stream.
Merrily, merrily, merrily, merrily,
Life is but a dream.

Row, row, row your boat
With a calm mentality;
Perform this with high spirits
For there's no objective reality.

Sally go round the sun,
Sally go round the moon,
Sally go round the chimney pots
On a Saturday afternoon.

Sally circumvent the star at the centre
of our solar system,
Sally circumvent the Earth's biggest
natural satellite,
Sally circumvent the
domestic smokestacks
Prior to Saturday night.

See, saw, Marjorie Daw,
Johnny shall have a new master.
He shall have but a penny a day,
Because he can't work any faster.

***

See, see! What shall I see?
A horse's head where his tail
should be.

See, saw, Marjorie Daw,
Johnny will be on the dole.
He shall have but a penny a day,
Because he's on a work-to-rule.

***

See, see! What shall I see?
An equine quadruped remodelled by
extensive plastic surgery.

Sing a song of sixpence,
A pocket full of rye;
Four and twenty blackbirds
Baked in a pie.
When the pie was opened,
They all began to sing.
Now, wasn't that a dainty dish
To set before the King?

Vocalize re: several coins,
A pouch with cereal grass replete;
Twenty-four Icteridae,
Encased in dough, exposed to heat.
The crusty membrane then
was breached,
The birds proceeded to cantate;
What a delicate oblation
To bestow upon a potentate.

Six little mice sat down to spin,
Pussy passed by and she peeped in.
What are you doing my little men?
Weaving coats for gentlemen.
Shall I come in and cut off
your tails?
No, no Mistress Pussy, you would
bite off our heads.
Oh, no, I'll not;
I'll help you to spin.
That may be so, but best
don't come in.

*Resting vertically with buttocks
providing support, it is said,
Six little mice were drawing out and
twisting fibres into thread.
They told a curious cat that their
sartorial industry
Was for male members of
the aristocracy.
The cat then offered tail amputation,
Which they politely declined, fearing
immediate decapitation;
Her subsequent offer of
spinning assistance,
Was likewise met with
sceptical resistance.*

Star light, star bright,
First star I see tonight,
I wish I may, I wish I might,
Have the wish I wish tonight.

***

Tell-tale tit,
Your tongue shall be slit,
And all the dogs in the town
Shall have a little bit.

Celestial body of high illumination,
The first to come to my observation,
May my strong desire or inclination,
Be given immediate validation.

***

Tiny gossiping warm-blooded,
egg-laying, feathered vertebrate,
Your lingua we will lacerate,
And among all the canine domesticated
carnivorous mammals in the town
The fleshy gobbets we shall circulate.

Eight fingers, ten toes,
Two eyes, and one nose.
Baby said when she smelt the rose,
'Oh! what a pity
I've only one nose.'

Ten teeth in even rows,
Three dimples, and one nose.
Baby said when she smelt the snuff,
'Deary me! one nose is enough.'

The Difference

Eight manual and ten pedal digits,
Two visual and one olfactory organ.
The scent of the ornamental flower
with leaves pinnately compound
Caused the infant to expound with
some distress
Her perceived lack of smelling apparatus.

Ten hard, bonelike structures rooted in
sockets of the jaw
Three small natural indentations in the
flesh of the cheek
And a proboscis.
The infant said when she inhaled a
finely-pulverized tobacco sample,
'Deary me! One nozzle should be ample.'

Oh, the grand old Duke of York,
He had ten thousand men;
He marched them up to the top of
the hill,
And he marched them down again.

And, when they were up they
were up;
And when they were down they
were down.
But when they were only
halfway up,
They were neither up nor down.

The Grand Old Duke of York

Oh, the grand old Duke of York,
He had ten thousand men;
He marched them up to the top of
the acclivity,
And he marched them down
the declivity.

And, when they were up they were up;
And when they were down they
were down.
But when they were equidistant to
these two fixed points,
They were neither of the
aforementioned.

The Lion and the Unicorn
Were fighting for the crown;
The Lion beat the Unicorn
All about the town.
Some gave them white bread
And some gave them brown;
Some gave them plum cake
And drummed them out of town!

For a diadem, the Lion and
the Unicorn
Engaged in pugnacious confrontation.
The former subjected the latter to a
mobile humiliation.
Some offered the carnivore and single-
horned mythical beast
Baked leavened flour first mixed
with yeast;
Others offered fruitcake but the
inevitable upshot
Was the imposition of a
municipal boycott.

The man in the moon
Came down too soon,
And asked the way to Norwich;
He went by the South
And burnt his mouth
With supping cold plum porridge.

*The man who dwells on the Orb
of Night
Was ill-advised to expedite
His journey to East Anglia.
On his southerly tack
A cold oatmeal snack
Damaged his oral ganglia.*

The north wind doth blow,
And we shall have snow,
And what will poor robin do then,
Poor thing?
He'll sit in a barn,
And keep himself warm,
And hide his head under his wing,
Poor thing.

*Northerly squalls are prevalent in the
lower atmosphere;
Frozen precipitation will soon appear.
Consider poor robin's limited options.
What a wretched creature.
In a farm building he will
remain sedentary.
His head he will then secrete
Beneath his feather-covered modified
forelimb to preserve body heat.
What a wretched creature.*

The Queen of Hearts,
She made some tarts
All on a summer's day.
The Knave of Hearts,
He stole the tarts
And took them clean away.
The King of Hearts,
Called for the tarts
And beat the Knave full sore.
The Knave of Hearts,
Brought back the tarts
And vowed he'd steal no more.

The Queen of Hearts,
She made some tarts
All on a summer's day.
The Knave of Hearts
Broke his parole
When those tarts he stole.
The King of Hearts
Punished this direption
By administering punitive flagellation,
Which caused the Knave of Hearts
To remonstrate
That he would never recidivate.

There was a little turtle
Who lived in a box.
He swam in the puddles
And climbed on the rocks.
He snapped at the mosquito,
He snapped at the flea.
He snapped at the minnow,
And he snapped at me.
He caught the mosquito,
He caught the flea.
He caught the minnow,
But he didn't catch me!

There Was A Little Turtle

In a container constructed with four
sides perpendicular to the base
as its domicile,
Lived a bony-shelled aquatic
(or terrestrial) reptile.
In a small pool of rainwater it
performed natation,
And moved upwards on a natural
mineral aggregate formation.
It brought its jaws together briskly,
In an attempt to ensnare
two insects and a fish and me:
The latter unsuccessfully.

There was an old crow
Sat upon a clod;
That's the end of my song,
That's odd!

There was a Corvus as old as the dawn
of time,
With his torso vertical and his body
supported on his buttock;
That's the end of my rhyme,
How idiosyncratic!

There was an old woman who lived
in a shoe,
She had so many children she
didn't know what to do;
She gave them some broth without
any bread;
She whipped them all soundly and
put them to bed.

In a durable covering for human feet,
Lived a female uterine
endurance athlete.
But her advancing years and prolonged
propagative success
Had led to overcrowding of her abode
and inevitable distress.
No brioche would sustain her
unruly brood:
Consommé was their staple food.
When each child had been
inadequately fed,
She'd administer correction and send
them all to bed.

Three blind mice, see how they run!
They all ran after the farmer's wife,
Who cut off their tails with a
carving knife,
Did you ever see such a sight in
your life,
As three blind mice?

*Oh! Mus musculi! Tragic trio with
obliquity of sight,
How glorious the alacrity with which
they take flight!
Until the helpmate of he who tills the
earth with zeal
Abscinded three funicular tails with
cold denticulated steel.
Have you ever attended a scene with so
transcendent an appeal
As Mus musculi? Tragic trio with
obliquity of sight.*

Here come three jolly, jolly
sailor boys
Just lately come for shore;
They spend their time in a merry,
merry way
Just as they did before !

A trio of blithe young mariners
Have completed debarkation;
They enjoy high-spirited dalliance
As on a previous occasion.

To market, to market, to buy a
fat pig,
Home again, home again,
jiggety-jig.
To market, to market, to buy a
fat hog,
Home again, home again,
jiggety-jog.

*To indulge our preference for
corpulent porkers,
We travel where commodities are
offered by hawkers.
Then, jerkily bobbing along the road,
We retreat to the comfort of our
native abode.
To indulge our preference for a
corpulent boar
We employ a similar method to that
used before.*

Tom, Tom, the piper's son,
Stole a pig, and away did run!
The pig was eat,
And Tom was beat,
And Tom went crying
Down the street.

Tom, Tom, the piper's son,
Stole Parma Ham and away did run!
His porcine malefaction
Attracted punitive action.
His eyes with briny globules o'erflowed
While he ambulated down the road.

Tweedle-dum and Tweedle-dee
Resolved to have a battle,
For Tweedle-dum said Tweedle-dee
Had spoiled his nice new rattle.

Just then flew by a monstrous crow,
As big as a tar barrel,
Which frightened both the
heroes so,
They quite forgot their quarrel.

Tweedle-dum and Tweedle-dee
Agreed to military engagement,
For Tweedle-dum said Tweedle-dee
Had blighted his novel percussive
equipment.

Then appeared a monolithic Corvus
As massive as a barrel for
hydrocarbon distillation,
Which made those Alpha males so
inordinately nervous
That they became insensible of their
previous altercation.

Two little dickie birds sitting
on a wall,
One named Peter, one named Paul.
Fly away Peter, fly away Paul;
Come back Peter, come back Paul.

*A brace of egg-laying, feathered
vertebrates called Peter and Paul,
Resting vertically with buttocks
providing support, on a wall.
Sally forth in aviation,
Then execute a speedy remigration.*

Wee Willie Winkie
Runs through the town,
Upstairs and downstairs,
In his nightgown.
Rapping at the window,
Crying through the lock,
'Are the children in their beds?
Now it's eight o'clock.'

Wee Willie Winkie's
obsessive condition
Expresses itself in this
unnecessary mission:
Every night at eight o'clock
He noisily upholds a curfew, and
likes to knock
On the window of every
child's domicile;
Though psychiatric treatment would be
more worthwhile.

Where, Oh where has my little
dog gone?
Oh where, Oh where can he be?
With his hair cut short and his tail
cut long
Oh where, Oh where can he be?

***

Had a mule, his name was Jack,
I rode his tail to save his back;
His tail got loose and I fell back;
Whoa, Jack!

My diminutive bristly
long-tailed hound
Is not to be found.

***

Had a beast of burden, his
name was Jack,
I rode his posterior appendage to
preserve his sacroiliac.
It came loose and I fell back;
Show some restraint, Jack!

Yankee Doodle came to town,
A-ridin' on a pony;
He stuck a feather in his hat
And called it macaroni.

***

Yankee Doodle came to town,
Displaying equestrian skill;
With a pasta illusion in his hat
Created with a quill.